Quentin Blake

MISTER
MAGNOLIA

COLLINS
PICTURE LIONS

First published in Great Britain by
Jonathan Cape Ltd in 1980
First published in Picture Lions in 1981
This edition published in 1992
10 9 8 7 6 5 4 3 2
Picture Lions is an imprint
of the Children's Division,
part of HarperCollins Publishers Limited,
77-85 Fulham Palace Road, Hammersmith,
London W6 8JB

Produced by HarperCollins Hong Kong

Mr Magnolia has only one boot.

He has an old trumpet

that goes rooty-toot —

And two lovely sisters

who play on the flute —

But Mr Magnolia has only one boot.

In his pond live a frog

and a toad and a newt —

He has green parakeets

who pick holes in his suit —

And some very fat owls
who are learning to hoot —
But Mr Magnolia
has only one boot.

He gives rides to his friends

when he goes for a scoot —

And the splash is immense
when he comes down
the chute —

But Mr Magnolia
has only one boot.

Just look at the way that

he juggles with fruit!

The mice all march past

as he takes the salute!

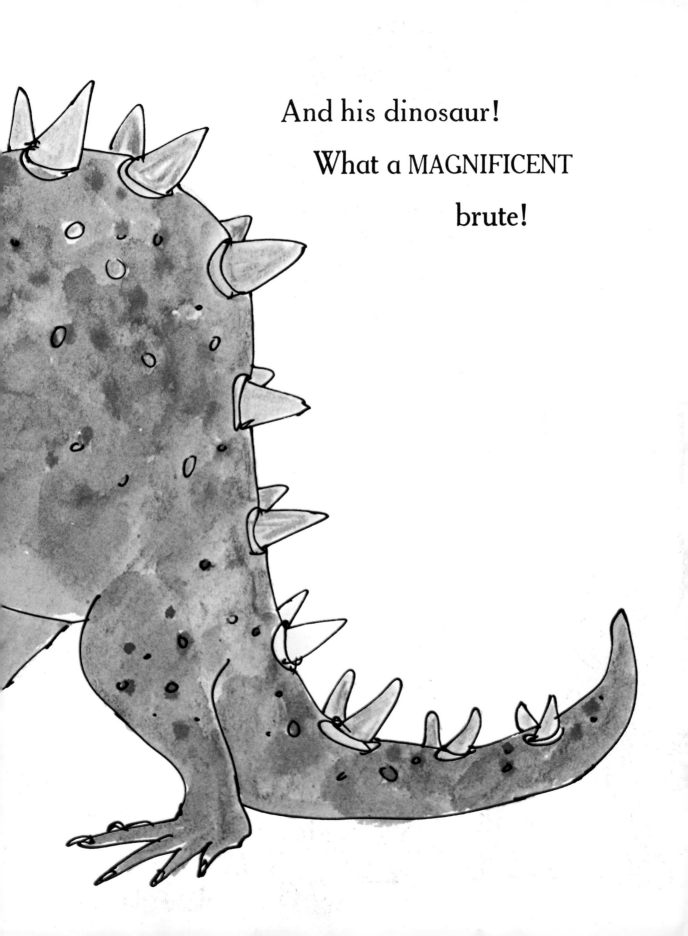

And his dinosaur!

What a MAGNIFICENT

brute!

But Mr Magnolia —
poor Mr Magnolia!
— Mr Magnolia
has
only one boot . . .

Hey —

Wait a minute . . .

Now then . . .

Keep going . . .

What's this?

Look!

It's a boot!

It's a boot!

Whoopee
for Mr Magnolia's
new boot!

Good night.